Amari's Book Report

Written by
Ginelle Wynter

Illustrated by
May Shamis

First paperback edition, 2020

Edited by Lily Mordaunt
Illustrated by May Shamis
Book Design by IAPS.rocks

ISBN 978-0-578-76970-7 (paperback)
ISBN 978-0-578-76971-4 (ebook)

Dedication

For Akilah, whose curious eyes and
kind heart are worth the world.
And for my grandad, Roy, my favorite storyteller.

"ALRIGHT EVERYONE," MS. BOYK CALLED out to her 4th grade class, "before we go, take out your vacation packet and let's talk about your assignment."

Ms. Boyk was Amari's favorite teacher. She was tall and slim but looked strong enough to lift two desks over her head easily. She always spoke kindly to her students and encouraged them to talk about their ideas with each other instead of just telling them what to do all day like a drill sergeant. Ms. Boyk had short curly hair and always wore the most interesting earrings Amari had ever seen.

"But, it's only a book report! We do these all the time," replied Akilah, the beads in her hair click clacking as she shook her head.

"Oh no, this is not like any book report you've completed before," the teacher smiled. "For this report, you'll be writing about your family!"

The students looked at each other, eyebrows raised, and broke into a buzz. "But Ms. Boyk," Eli raised his hand, pushing his glasses up his nose. "I don't know anyone famous in my family. We're not in any books."

"Exactly!" Ms. Boyk beamed. "And you're going to change that. Your assignment is to write about your family stories, as if it was a book. In the packet, I gave you several questions that you can ask your relatives to gather details. I want you to talk to a couple of different people in your family. Then, use the details that you gather to write a short story. Your packet also reviews the steps that we've used in the past to write stories. Any questions?"

The murmurs in the classroom grew louder as the students turned to each other with new questions. Akilah raised her hand, her bracelets clattering together, "but how will we know which details to choose?"

"Thank you for raising your hand this time," Ms. Boyk replied, looking around at her students. "That choice is up to you. I want you to learn that you don't have to go to the movies or the library to find a great story. You can hear fascinating stories from the people you see at home every day. In fact, I'm sure you've already heard plenty of stories from your family members, especially during the holidays. I want you to spend time asking your relatives to tell you those stories again. You may be surprised by how many new things you learn."

Just then, the bell rang, "When we return, you will share your stories with the class, and work with your classmates to edit them before we publish your final products. Have a great vacation everyone! I'm excited to read your stories when we return!"

The students packed up their backpacks and bounced with excitement out of the classroom and off to their vacation. Amari walked out with Eli, his best friend since the first grade, talking about plans for their sleepover next weekend. Eli's family had invited Amari to join their trip to Six Flags and they both looked forward to stuffing themselves full of cotton candy.

Amari spotted his mom's signature blue scarf, wrapped around her long kinky hair. She was waiting near the door to the schoolyard, holding her mobility cane out of the way of the passing crowd. He rushed over to meet her, wrapping his arms around her side in a tight hug.

"Squeeze!" he yelled, giggling as his mom returned the hug.

"Hey bud," her round face lit up with a smile, "you're getting stronger every day! Who's feeding you?" They laughed together.

Even though he was only eight years old, Amari was already almost as tall as his mom. Where his mom was petite, Amari was growing tall like his dad, but skinnier.

"How was school?" she asked, as they began the short walk home.

"Science class was really fun. We had a team competition to see who could build the tallest spaghetti tower that could hold a marshmallow at the top," he explained. "Oh! And Ms. Boyk gave us a book report. I'm going to write a story about you!"

Amari explained what Ms. Boyk had just told the class, hopping along on the sidewalk as he talked.

"That sounds like a lot of fun," his mom replied, her cane tapping alongside Amari. "But there are so many interesting stories about the family. Maybe you should talk to a few other relatives before you choose?"

Amari shrugged, he didn't think anyone could be cooler than his mom, but he agreed to give it a try.

The next day after breakfast, Amari got right to work. He turned on his phone and called his grandad.

"Good morning, Gramps! Are you still coming to pick me up today?" he asked.

"Morning, son. I'm putting on my shoes now. Are you ready?" His grandad replied. "Yes, Gramps. I'll see you soon!"

After hanging up, Amari went over to his mirror to brush his hair. His dad was letting him grow out the top of his hair, but cut the sides low, so he could look like his favorite soccer player. He packed his phone, notebook, and pencil into his backpack. He kissed his mom goodbye and went outside to wait on the porch with his dad who was chatting with the neighbor about their shared garden.

"Good morning, Dad. Good morning, Ms. Kay," Amari chimed.

"Morning," his dad replied. "Where are you headed off to so early?"

"I'm hanging out with Gramps today so we can talk about my book report," Amari answered.

Just then, Amari spotted his grandad's green Jeep coming down the block. "Gotta run, Pop. See you later!" he called over his shoulder as he headed to the car.

"Hey, Gramps," Amari beamed, kissing his Grandad on the cheek through his peppery gray beard. "Where are we off to today?"

"Well," Gramps replied, "I want to stop by the bakery to pick up some saltfish patties and sweet bread, and then we can take a drive down to Coney Island. How's that?"

"Let's go!" Amari exclaimed, snapping his seatbelt into place. He loved stopping by Mr. Allen's Bake Shop. He always got an extra treat to take home.

As the Jeep rolled along Linden Boulevard, Amari opened up his notebook. His grandad always told stories while he drove, so all he had to do was wait.

And maybe it was the calypso music playing through the stereo this time, but it wasn't long before Gramps started to tell stories about the band he played in as a young man back in St. Vincent and the Grenadines. Amari had heard this story many times before but wrote down as many details as he could.

Through a broad nostalgic smile, Gramps talked about playing the drums late into the night with his bandmates, his long dreads hanging loose around his shoulders.

"Did you ever travel with your band?" Amari asked.

"Yea, sometimes we went to Barbados or Trinidad, but mostly, we played in our town," Gramps replied. "But I got to see a lot more countries when I was in the Navy."

Amari perked up to take notes about this new story.

"We went to Alaska, spent a while in Germany, Costa Rica, we saw a lot of different places," Gramps continued. "Those fellas on the ship would love when it was my turn to cook. One time, I made a big pot of pelau." He opened his arms wide to show the size of the pot as they waited in line at the bakery.

"I turned around to pick up a plate, and by the time I turned back, the whole pot was empty!" At that, Gramps threw his head back and broke into deep, shoulder shaking laughter. Amari loved his grandad's laugh, even in line with everyone watching. It always made Amari feel like he told the funniest jokes in the world.

By the time he got home that evening, Amari had pages full of notes about his grandad's adventures in the Navy. Ms. Boyk was right, he really could write a book with all these new stories.

Now, Amari was even more excited about what he might learn from Aunty Mae. She was coming over tomorrow to help make Sunday dinner. He loved spending time with his aunt. She always took him to explore new things around the city, so he was sure she'd have exciting stories to tell too.

The next afternoon, Amari sat at the kitchen table explaining his assignment to Aunty Mae. Her legs were folded onto the chair under her flowing orange skirt. Her hair was long and kinky, a lot like Amari's mom's hair, but Aunty Mae had streaks of light brown all over her afro. She looked over the packet Ms. Boyk had given the class as Amari talked, and when he finished, she smiled and said, "Okay! What do you want to start with?"

"Well," Amari pondered, "did you and mommy grow up in this neighborhood?"

"Actually," Aunty Mae replied, "I wasn't born in Brooklyn like your mom. I was born in Kingstown, Saint Vincent. I lived there with great-grandma, Olive, until I was eight. When she moved to London to live with Tanty Sharon, I moved to NY to live with grandma and your mom, and I've lived here ever since!"

"You didn't live with your mom growing up? I didn't know that." Amari said with surprise. He had a hard time imagining what life would be like without seeing his mom every day. "Did you miss her?"

"Yea, sometimes," she replied thoughtfully. "But growing up, it felt normal. Mom did visit when she could, and we talked on the phone every week. But I loved living with Granny Olive. She taught me to cook and bake, and we would take trips to the market every weekend. She would let me roam from stall to stall picking up ingredients for dinner. And sometimes we would pick up fruits to eat at the beach while we walked along the water," Aunty Mae smiled as she remembered.

"So that's how you learned to bake all those treats!" Amari replied. "Did you ever travel with Granny Olive?" He asked.

"No, we didn't travel much. But I do love to travel now. You know that," she winked.

"Can you tell me about one of your favorite trips?" Amari asked.

"Of course," Aunty Mae brightened. She told him about her recent trip to the coastal city Cartagena, Colombia. Her favorite memory on that trip was visiting a historic town called San Basilio de Palenque.

The town had been formed by escaped African slaves brought to Colombia by the Spanish. They successfully fought for their freedom and had preserved their African culture to this day. The most fascinating thing of all, Aunty Mae told him, was learning that women would corn-braid intricate map routes into their hair to help guide escaped slaves to the free town.

Amari was astonished. Aunty Mae had not told him this story before. When he got back to school, he would have to ask Ms. Boyk if the class could learn more about the history of the town, Palenque.

Aunty Mae continued to tell him stories about her trips around the world as she began to prepare dinner. Before bed that night, Amari looked back through his notes marveling at so many of the things he'd learned that day. It made him even more excited for his final interview with his mom.

Amari spent the next few days enjoying his spring vacation. He helped his dad in the garden in the mornings, went out to ride his scooter at the park with some of his school friends most afternoons, and at night, he sprawled out on his bed drawing pictures to illustrate the stories he'd heard from Gramps and Aunty Mae.

Amari waited as patiently as he could for a chance to interview his mom. She was working on finishing her own book by an upcoming editor's deadline. Amari's mom was an author, and in his opinion, she told the best stories of anyone he knew.

One morning after breakfast, Amari tiptoed down to his mom's home office and gently knocked on the door.

"Yes?" His mom called from her desk.

Amari peeked around the door. "I made you some tea," he smiled as he pushed the door open and carefully placed the tea on her desk.

"Thank you," his mom replied. "I could use a break," she said, rolling her wrists and stretching her fingers. "Why don't we take a walk through the park?" She asked, resting back in her chair. "And I can tell you a few stories for your book report."

"Ok!" Amari half-shouted, bouncing on his toes. "I'll go get dressed!" He added, before racing off to his room.

Amari's mom met him at the front door a few minutes later. He laced up his shoes and grabbed his phone. His mom had given him the good idea that he should make a voice recording while they walked since it would be hard to write on the move. His mom grabbed her mobility cane and keychain, and they headed out the door.

As they walked along their favorite path through Prospect Park, Amari's mom began her first story. "Have I told you about the last time I sang Christmas carols at the Metropolitan Museum?"

"No," Amari shook his head, listening eagerly. His mom had a beautiful voice. She was a chorus member at the music school that she had been a part of since she was six-years-old. It was a music program for musicians of all ages who were also visually impaired.

"Every Christmas, our chorus would carol at different locations around the city. We sang in office buildings, near Lincoln Center, and outside coffee shops. But the Met was always my favorite place to sing because of the way the sound bounced off the high ceilings of the museum," his mom shared. "And I met some of my best friends at the music school."

She went on to tell him about the many adventures she found herself in with her friends, including the time that they trained together for a half-marathon with the Road Runners Club.

"You ran a half marathon!?" Amari asked, surprised. He always thought of his dad as the athlete in the family.

"I did!" His mom replied. "I was a lot younger then, with much more energy than I have now," she laughed. "It's one of my proudest memories."

She told him about the challenges of training for so many months in all different types of weather, and that she had almost given up. But in the end, her friends helped her push through to the finish.

Amari's mom continued to tell her stories as they started to walk back home. Amari listened attentively asking for more details about these new stories.

By the time he got home, Amari had no idea where to begin his book report. He had learned so many amazing new things about his family that it made him start to think of who else in the family he could hear exciting new stories from.

But one thing Amari knew for sure was his family's stories were as good as any book.

Record your Family's Stories

Do you want to gather stories from your family like Amari did? Use the questions on the following pages to help you get started. Copy the questions into a notebook if you need more space or want to talk to more than one family member!

Family member's name:

_____

Draw what they look like or place a photo of them below.

Where were you born, and where did you grow up?

_____

_____

_____

_____

_____

_____

_____

_____

_____

_____

_____

_____

_____

Tell me about where you have lived.

_____

_____

_____

_____

_____

_____

_____

_____

_____

_____

_____

_____

_____

_____

What places have you visited?

Tell me about one of your funniest memories.

_____

_____

_____

_____

_____

_____

_____

_____

_____

_____

_____

_____

_____

_____

Tell me about your proudest memory.

_____

_____

_____

_____

_____

_____

_____

_____

_____

_____

_____

_____

_____

_____

Tell me something you experienced that was unbelievable.

_____

_____

_____

_____

_____

_____

_____

_____

_____

_____

_____

_____

_____

_____

Illustrate your stories here!

Illustrate your stories here!

Illustrate your stories here!

About the Author

Ginelle Wynter was born and raised in a Caribbean community in the heart of Brooklyn, NY. Growing up, she always loved gathering with friends and family to share stories into the late hours of the night. Having taught in NYC public schools for 5 years, she encouraged her students to stay connected to their community and express their cultural pride. At the start of each school year, she fostered connection in her classroom by inviting her students to share the significance of their favorite family recipe. As a new author she hopes to uplift stories that celebrate diverse cultures, family traditions, and community.

In her spare time, Ginelle enjoys Olympic style weightlifting, trying new foods, and traveling to explore new countries. Learn more by visiting ginellewynter.com

CPSIA information can be obtained
at www.ICGtesting.com
Printed in the USA
BVHW022256040121
596925BV00001BA/1